For the child I was and the child you are—
hope, healing, love, light —S.G.

To Francisco, with all my love —L.U.

Text copyright © 2022 by Sara Greenwood
Jacket art and interior illustrations copyright © 2022 by Luisa Uribe

Visit us on the web! rhcbooks.com

Educators and librarians, for a variety of teaching tools, visit us at RHTeachersLibrarians.com

Library of Congress Cataloging-in-Publication Data is available upon request.
ISBN 978-0-593-12716-2 (trade) — ISBN 978-0-593-12717-9 (lib. bdg.) — ISBN 978-0-593-12718-6 (ebook)

The text of this book is set in 16-point Weiss BT.
The illustrations were rendered in Photoshop.
Book design by Rachael Cole

MANUFACTURED IN CHINA
10 9 8 7 6 5 4 3 2 1
First Edition

MY BROTHER IS AWAY

BY **SARA GREENWOOD**

ILLUSTRATED BY **LUISA URIBE**

RANDOM HOUSE STUDIO
NEW YORK

My brother doesn't live here. He's far away.

Sometimes I stand in his quiet room and pretend he's not really gone. He's only with friends. He'll be home soon.

He used to carry me on his shoulders, the thump of his footsteps firm on the road as moonlight brightened our path. The sky stretched above, a field where stars bloomed. "Silly goose," he'd say when I tried to reach them, but he always held me steady.

"Where's your brother been?" a boy at the bus stop asks. "I haven't seen him around."

I want to say he's taken a job. Or he's learning to scuba dive. Or he's touring the world in a hot-air balloon. "He's busy," I say. Any lie is easier than the truth.

My brother told me stories. Sometimes he'd read them from books. Sometimes they came straight from his head. "Did you know?" he'd begin, and I'd snuggle close, cozy as a caterpillar in her cocoon.

"I saw your brother on the news," says a girl at school. "He did something bad." I want to fly away, fly so far I can forget what's happened. I want to travel high enough that the earth is only a speck and I'm friends with the moon.

Why did my brother do that awful thing?
I want to shout at him, "This is all your fault!"
I run to my room and slam the door—*wham*!

I curl up on my bed.

The door cracks open. Mama peeks in.

Daddy kisses my head. They say we'll see my brother soon. But still my chest squeezes tight.

Together, my brother and I flew my kite. He showed
me how to grip the string against the wind's tugging.
The kite swooped and sailed, its tail a rippling stream.

I stand in the yard and stare at the sky—so big, so empty.

Those afternoons feel like a faraway dream.

Mama helps me count the days. One morning she asks,

"Are you ready?"

Daddy drives us a whole world away—

down winding roads,

over bridges and hills,

through cloudbursts and sunshine,

past towns and trains . . .

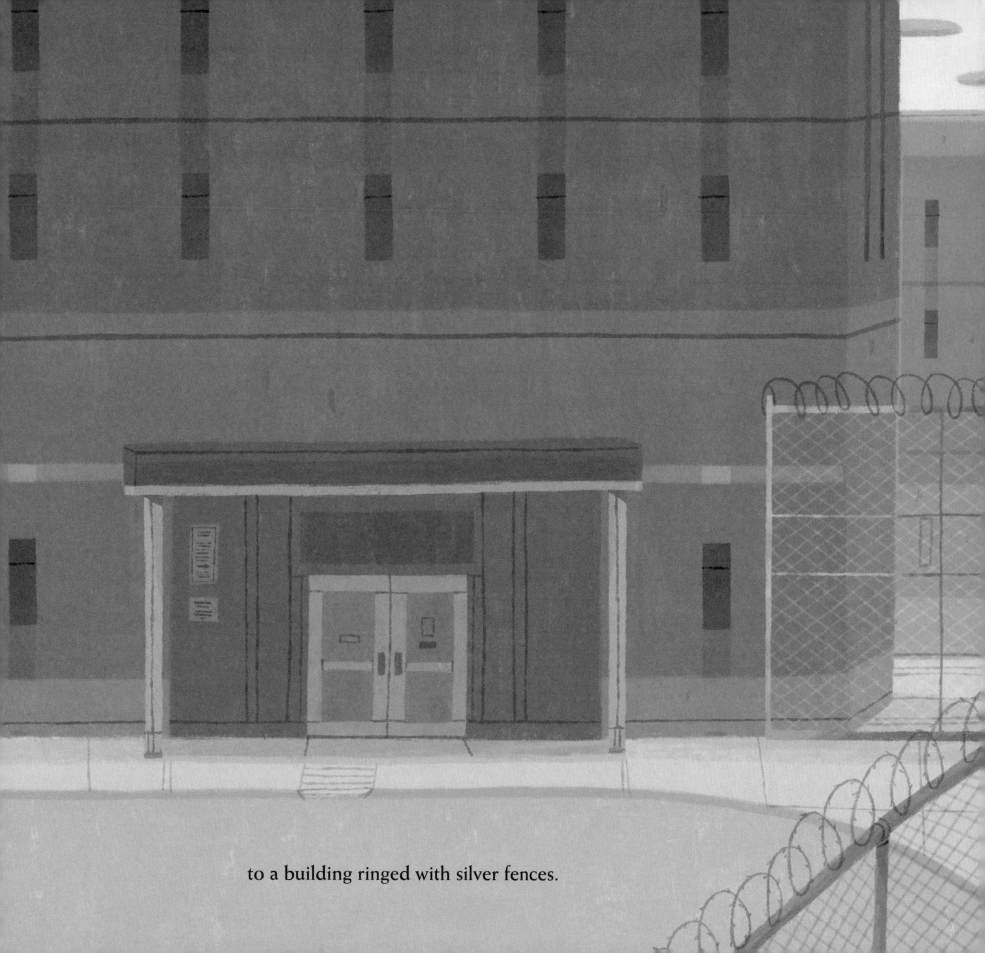

to a building ringed with silver fences.

We push inside.

We stand in line.

Do I look the same? Have I grown since he left?

Will my brother remember me?

I watch the door—ready.

Finally, I see him. His smile says he's seen me, too.

"There's my silly goose." My brother pulls me close.
"Did you know I've been waiting for you?"

Everything is different. Everything is the same.
My brother's not home, but his love hasn't changed.

I see
I'm not the only one
whose brother is away.

AUTHOR'S NOTE

For much of my childhood, my brother and I lived apart. He was arrested when I was in first grade and released from prison when I was in eighth. I didn't know anyone with a family like mine. There were times I felt sad. Other times I felt embarrassed. Some days I was angry. Often, I was lonely and confused. These feelings were upsetting. Later I learned they were perfectly normal for kids like me.

Many families are unable to regularly visit their loved ones in prison, but I was lucky. Several times a year, my family drove nearly five hundred miles to spend time with my brother. It took eight hours to reach him. During visiting hours we talked, we told stories, and we played card games. We felt like a family again. At the prison, I saw other kids visiting their relatives. For the first time I realized I wasn't alone. There were other families like mine.

If someone you love is in prison, I want you to know you aren't alone, either. I hope this book feels like a friend.

CLASS PICTURE OF THE
AUTHOR IN FIRST GRADE